The LOST BOY and the MONSTER

by **Craig Kee Strete**

paintings by **Steve Johnson** and **Lou Fancher**

G. P. Putnam's Sons ◎ New York

Old Foot Eater was an awful old monster. Even other monsters said so. His teeth were hard as stone, his eyes were as big and bulgy

Well, my goodness, he liked to eat little children's feet!

He lived in an old medicine basket atop a hollow tree.
He kept a long sticky rope hanging down from his tree. It was
all tangled and snarled and looped around and around.

The monster liked it that way. Because any child foolish enough to walk beneath his tree was sure to get his foot caught.

When that happened, the monster did not call it an accident, he called it lunch.

In a forest not too far away lived a lost boy who had no name. He had had a name once, but because he was lost and so seldom talked to anyone, he forgot it.

One day the lost boy came walking toward the tree where the foot-eating monster lived. The boy saw a rattlesnake sitting in the sun. He did not see the monster's sticky rope tangled and angled and looped every which way.

The rattlesnake lowered his head and tried to hide, but the lost boy saw him anyway.

"Aren't you going to hit me with a stick?" asked the rattlesnake. "Most people do the minute they see me."

"Why should I do that?" said the lost boy. "Snakes belong in this world just like me."

The snake said, "I thank you for letting me be me. I name you Snake Brother," and the lost boy walked past the snake.

The lost boy saw a scorpion drying his tail in the sun. The lost boy did not see the monster's sticky rope coiled and oiled and looped every which way. The scorpion tried to pull back under a rock, but the lost boy saw him anyway.

"Aren't you going to hit me with a stick?" asked the scorpion. "Most people do the minute they see me."

"Why should I do that?" said the lost boy. "Scorpions have their place in the world just like me."

The scorpion said, "I thank you for letting me be me. I name you Scorpion Brother," and the lost boy walked past the scorpion.

And then the lost boy stepped on the sticky-icky rope.
It stuck fast to the bottom of his foot. When he tried to kick it
loose, his other foot stuck to it too.

The more he struggled, the more tangled up he got. And just when he thought things couldn't get any worse, somebody began pulling on the rope!

The lost boy found himself being pulled up to the top of a big old tree.

"What have we here?" said the foot-eating monster with a huge hungry smile.

"I'm stuck in this rope. Could you please help me get free?"

"I'd be happy to help you out of that rope," said the monster. He moved carefully so that he did not touch the rope himself, and with his great monster strength he pulled the boy free from the rope. The rope dropped back down toward the bottom of the tree, ready to

"Thank you for saving me," said the lost boy.

"I think I deserve a reward for saving you," said the monster.
"How about a nice lunch?"

"I'd be glad to give you lunch, but I don't have any food with me," said the lost boy.

"Oh yes you do. You're standing on them!" said the monster, and he grabbed the boy and put him in a huge cooking pot. "I'm going to the river to get some water so you can soak your feet. That makes them nice and tender," said the monster with a greedy laugh.

The monster climbed down a ladder nailed to the back of the tree.

The lost boy jumped as high as he could, but he could not reach the rim of the cooking pot. He was trapped.

Then he heard a slithering sound and a hissing sound.

He looked up. Along the rim of the pot, something moved.

"Don't worry," hissed a voice. "I the rattlesnake will help you."
The snake held tight to the rim of the pot with his tail and then
let his head hang down into the pot.

"Climb up my body," said the rattlesnake. "Then you can
get away."

The lost boy was glad he shared the world with the rattlesnake.
Using the snake as a rope, he managed to climb up out of the
cooking pot.

"Now you can climb down the tree ladder," said the snake.
The lost boy thanked the rattlesnake for his help and climbed

When he reached the bottom, a rock moved and the scorpion crawled out from under it. The scorpion held a small medicine bag in his claws. "Take this. It is the poison from my sting. If danger threatens, drop it behind you." The scorpion smiled at him. "It is a gift from scorpion wisdom."

The lost boy took the medicine bag and was glad he had made
friends with the scorpion.
He turned and began to run as fast as his legs would carry him.

But just then the monster was coming back from the river. The monster saw the lost boy and began to run after him. The earth shook as his mighty feet hit the ground.

When the monster was about to catch him, the lost boy threw the

When the sting hit the ground, it turned into a desert of thick spiny cactus and the monster ran right into it and fell into the stickers.

The stickers stuck him everywhere, and the monster howled with pain. He could not chase the boy with all the stickers in his feet.

The lost boy with two names got away, and from that day on he never felt lost again.

Old Foot Eater limped home and was so angry that he forgot about
the sticky-icky rope and stepped right on it. He tossed and turned
and roared and screamed, but the sticky-icky rope stuck to his nose

And to this day, they say he is stuck there still.

Text copyright © 1999 by Craig Kee Strete
Illustrations copyright © by Steve Johnson and Lou Fancher
All rights reserved. This book, or parts thereof, may
not be reproduced in any form without permission in
writing from the publisher, G. P. Putnam's Sons, a
division of Penguin Putnam Books for Young Readers,
345 Hudson Street, New York, NY 10014.
G. P. Putnam's Sons, Reg. U.S. Pat. & Tm. Off.
Published simultaneously in Canada. Printed in Hong Kong
by South China Printing Co. (1988) Ltd.
Text set in Tiepolo Book

Library of Congress Cataloging-in-publication Data
Strete, Craig. The lost boy and the monster / Craig Kee Strete ;
illustrated by Steve Johnson and Lou Fancher.   p. cm.
Summary: With the help of a rattlesnake and a scorpion, a lost boy
gains two names and defeats the horrible foot-eating monster.
[1. Monsters—Fiction.   2. Rattlesnakes—Fiction.   3. Scorpions—Fiction.]
I. Johnson, Steve, 1960-   ill.   II. Fancher, Lou, ill.   III. Title.
PZ7.S9164Lo   1999 [E]—dc21 98-17333 CIP AC
ISBN 0-399-22922-1
1 3 5 7 9 10 8 6 4 2
First Impression

Designed by Lou Fancher

About The Art
The artwork for this book was inspired by Steve and Lou's
study of American Indian art, masks, basket weaving and sculpture.
They gathered information about cave paintings and researched
petroglyphs from the Southwest. The paintings were created on
canvas using a textured paste, oil paint, potato stamping,
and a wide variety of scratching tools.